SWEET OF
BETRAYAL

An Erotic Horror Novella

❦

HARLEIGH BECK

Author's Note

Hi, dear reader.

This erotic horror novella is not intended for readers under 18.
Trigger warnings include graphic murder, explicit sexual content, sexual violence, and dub/non-con that some readers might find upsetting/offensive. Please don't read this if any of that bothers you.

Now that's been said, let's jump down the rabbit hole.

CHAPTER 1

The air smells of a damp forest and early autumn evenings. I shut the car off and scan my eyes over the log cabin we've rented for the weekend while my friends, Maddy and Jess, squeal with excitement.

It'd been a long shot to ask my mom permission to let us rent a cabin for my eighteenth birthday, so imagine my surprise when she agreed.

"It's perfect!" Jess says, bouncing next to me, her brown hair moving in the afternoon breeze.

I'm more skeptical than her. The log cabin looks nothing like the website. It's rundown, framed by overgrown weeds and grass, and you can smell the rotten wood from here.

In the distance, a crow caws. A shiver runs down my back as Maddy opens the trunk.

"I can't believe my mom agreed to let me stay here," she says, hauling her overnight bag out.

Jess moves forward to collect hers. "There's no one around for miles. How much trouble can we get into?"

We laugh at that.

Maddy's heels sink into the grass as she makes her way to

the log cabin, dragging her excessive overnight bag with incredible difficulty.

I lift out my duffel bag and shut the trunk. Since we're away for one night, I haven't packed much—only the necessities.

"Are you coming?" Jess calls out, eager for me to unlock the door with the old key we collected.

The silence out here is deafening. At least it is until the tranquility is disturbed by the squeal of tires.

A red Honda parks next to my car, and Adam opens his door while his friends, Brian and Zach, file out. They're loud and boisterous, which is nothing new.

"What's up, ladies?" Adam beams, flashing me a smile over the car hood. He rounds the car, wraps his arm around my shoulder, and looks at the log cabin, his nose scrunching up. "False marketing. You should demand your money back."

"We're here now and parent-free. Let's make the most of it."

"That was going to be my next point," he replies, picking up my bag. "Ask for the refund *after* we've had the best weekend of our life."

I roll my eyes. He's a dork, albeit a good-looking one with a mass of brown, haywire hair. Dressed in a pair of light blue jeans and a black T-shirt, he looks casual, but anyone who's friends with Adam knows he takes great care in his looks. He doesn't just throw clothes on; he simply wants it to look like he does.

Brian, Maddy's boyfriend, peers through the window next to the front door while Zach looks bored. You could be at the top of a rollercoaster, and he would still look like he'd rather be anywhere else. The girls at school love his permanent scowl and the wisps of black hair sticking out from beneath his hood.

His brown eyes flick up to me briefly before focusing

back on the phone in his hand. We had sex once, a couple of months back, which the others don't know.

It happened when Adam and I broke up for the final time after I caught him cheating on me with a cheerleader at a party. I wasn't even angry, which took me by surprise. We'd been on and off for a year, breaking up for the silliest of reasons the way teenagers do. But when I walked in on him fucking another girl, I realized we were over for good. We're better off as friends.

That night, Zach found me out by the pool and walked me home. One thing led to another, and the next thing I knew, I was flat on my back in my bed with his head buried between my legs.

Not my proudest moment.

I join the girls on the porch and unlock the door. It creaks open, revealing a short hallway that opens up to an open plan living room and kitchen area.

The decrepit cabin smells of mildew and damp wood. When was the last time someone cracked a window open in this place?

I walk in and place my duffel bag down on the fabric couch. It has a tartan blanket draped over the back. Framed cross-stitched pictures hang on the walls along with a wooden cross with a crucified Jesus over the door. Everything about this place reminded me of my great-grandmother when she was alive.

The empty eyes of Jesus follow me as I walk up to the window and look out at the forest beyond.

"I'm checking out the bedrooms," Brian says, making a beeline for the stairs.

Maddy pinches a pillow between her finger and thumb, lifting it in the air. She wrinkles her nose. "Is there even any stuffing in this?"

"Don't be such a princess," Adam teases, plopping down on the couch, his foot on the coffee table.

She chucks the thin cushion at him, making him laugh. "Jerk!"

His eyes gleam as he looks up at me behind her.

The trees sway in the wind outside, and dried leaves painted a myriad of autumn colors blow along the grass.

I turn away from the window and attempt a weak smile. I invited my friends here; the least I can do is to faux excitement. "Let's check out the bedrooms."

"Is the TV working?" Jess asks, crouching down and pressing the power button. Nothing happens.

Zach, leaning against the wall, looks up from his phone. "Try plugging it in."

She blinks, then searches for the plug that lies spooled behind the TV. "Smartass."

Feet thunder on the stairs, and Brian appears in the doorway. "Shotgun on the main bedroom."

I roll my eyes and plop down next to Adam. A clock ticks somewhere. "Now what?"

He flashes me a wide grin, the kind I used to find charming but have grown immune to. "We drink."

Not one to miss out on alcohol, Brian is already rooting through the cupboards.

"What are you doing?" Adam asks, cupping his mouth.

Brian's head pops up behind the island. "The ladies want drinks, don't they?"

Jess has finally managed to get the TV working, but the signal here is terrible. She slams her hand down on the top. "Anyone up for a black and white western?"

Adam places his arm around my shoulder and pulls me closer.

He's still trying to get me back, but I'm not easily swayed.

Zach's eyes flick up from his phone again, tracking my movements as Adam sinks lower on the couch.

I break eye contact first. "Why is your arm around my shoulder?"

"Don't be like that," Adam replies with a mischievous smile. "You can't hold a grudge forever."

I give him an incredulous look. "Are you serious? You cheated on me, and now you're telling me not to hold a grudge?" Should I laugh or cry? It's a hard choice. His stupidity has reached new heights.

"You can't stay mad forever."

Apparently, it wasn't high enough.

"This is so fucking sweet!" Brian says, re-joining us with bowls in his hands. He holds them up. "For snacks."

Maddy wheels over the suitcase packed with food and unzips it. Inside is a selection of chips and bags of sweets. Everything that we would need for a stay overnight.

I help her fill the bowls and place them on the coffee table while Brian brings glasses from the kitchen area and unscrews the lid on the vodka bottle. "Get the lemonade," he tells Adam, who jumps up and helps Maddy unload the suitcase.

He returns with the drink and hands it to Brian.

"Thanks."

I wrinkle my nose as Brian pours vodka into the glass and fills it the rest of the way with lemonade. "That's a bit strong, isn't it?"

"It's half-and-half."

"Exactly."

He rolls his eyes and snatches the glass out of my hands. Then he offers it to Adam and says, "You're not a princess, are you?"

Adam takes a large swig, wincing, his voice squeaky. "Not at all."

I hide my amused smile behind my hand.

"Here you go, your royal highness," Brian says, handing me another glass. This time with far less vodka in it.

He tips the bottle in Zach's direction. "Do you want a drink?"

Zach nods slowly, not bothering with a verbal response.

I sweep my eyes down his black hoodie and ripped black jeans. His wallet is inside his front pocket, attached to a chain that dangles down his thigh.

I've never seen Zach wear a splash of color, which adds to his brooding persona.

His eyes meet mine, and I look away, taking another sip of my drink.

Jess smacks the top of the TV again as it starts flickering. "Shit reception."

"Have a drink." Brian holds a glass out for her, and she blows strands of raven hair from her face as she walks over. "Are you trying to get me drunk?"

"Babe," he teases, "we're in a log cabin, away from our overbearing parents. Of course, I'm trying to get you drunk!"

A smile plays over her lips.

Maddy plops down on the couch but straightens back up and helps herself to a Bon Bon. She pops it in her mouth and says, "It's too good to be true, isn't it? To think our parents agreed to us going away for a night?"

Brian shrugs one shoulder and joins her on the couch, his arm stretched out behind her. "My parents don't care as long as I don't get into trouble with the cops."

The sun is slowly setting outside, casting the room in a soft orange glow that makes the glasses look like they sparkle.

"Yeah, mine say the same," Adam butts in, grabbing a handful of chips. His words are muffled when he talks around a mouthful, "They're probably happy to have the house to themselves."

I stare at him in disgust. He has bits of crushed chips stuck to his bottom lip.

"What?" he asks, looking confused.

I scoff and walk past him to sit on the floor on the other side of the coffee table where the TV is at my back. The movie flickers and jumps on the screen. Jess has long since given up on making it work. She lowers herself down next to me. "My mom said no at first."

"What made her change her mind?" Adam asks, sitting down in the armchair. He reaches behind him and removes the sad excuse of a cushion, tossing it on the floor.

"She didn't."

A hush falls over the room.

"What do you mean?" I ask, my eyes wide.

"I snuck out."

Brian breaks the silence as he begins laughing. Adam soon joins in too, vodka spilling over the sides of his glass. "You'll be in so much fucking trouble when we get back."

"Yep," she agrees, taking a large gulp of her drink. "I couldn't let you guys have fun without me."

"Damn right!" Adam chimes in, raising his glass in the air for a toast. "Here's to be being rebellious teenagers."

While they toast, I peek over my shoulder at Zach. He's so different from his friends, always quiet and pensive, but you know nothing gets past him. His eyes clash with mine, and I avert my gaze as a blush creeps up my neck.

"Dude, sit down!" Brian says to him. "There's room on the couch."

"Or next to me on the floor." Jess pats the space. She's always had a thing for him, which makes me feel like a shit friend.

The sun slips behind the trees, taking the last daylight with it.

Jess gets to her feet and switches on a floor-standing lamp next to the TV. Her fruity perfume permeates the air when she sinks back down next to me.

Maddy leans forward, her eyes sparkling with excitement. "So, I researched this place, and it turns out there's a legend."

Adam rubs his hands together. "I fucking love a good legend!"

Maddy ignores him while Brian toys with her hair as she continues, "It's said that three masked men appear once every year to claim the blood of young souls. The people who've stayed here on the anniversary have never been seen again."

Brian's fingers pause their twirling in her hair. "Babe, you don't believe that shit, do you?"

She rolls her eyes and gives him a bored look. "For once in your life, don't spoil it."

Jess speaks up next to me. "When's the anniversary?"

A slow, mischievous smile unfurls on Maddy's lips. "Tonight."

Choking on my drink, I laugh. "That's so fucking stupid."

Maddy gives her boyfriend Brian a look. "You should date her. You can be boring together."

"What do they do?" Jess asks.

"They kill you."

"Yeah, but how?"

Maddy downs the last of her drink and places it on the coffee table. The flickering TV reflects in her blue eyes. "They come carrying weapons, and then they tie you up and play twisted games before killing you."

"But why?" Jess asks, always the curious one.

8

Maddy blows out a frustrated breath. "Never mind why! They just do. It's a legend."

"So a fairy tale," Zach speaks up behind me, his deep voice sending a tingle of goosebumps up my arms.

"I give up!" Maddy says, throwing her hands up helplessly before smacking her thighs. "You guys are no fun at all."

I take a large sip of my drink to conceal my smile.

"Babe," Brian tries to soothe her, rubbing her back, "you're too serious."

Jess isn't done with her line of questioning. "But why this place, and why this date? How do they even know there will be people here on this date every year?"

Maddy's mouth falls open, and she releases a strangled, disbelieving sound. "I read it on a website. It didn't go into details. Maybe they check the bookings beforehand."

"Who cares," Adam says, hopping to his feet. "I vote we play spin the bottle."

"What's next? Seven minutes in heaven?" Jess laughs next to me. "Aren't we too old for these games?"

Adam waves her off and picks up the vodka bottle. "Come on, gather around."

Brian gets to his feet and pulls a reluctant Maddy up by her hand. They're the only couple in the room, so it makes sense why she doesn't feel ecstatic about this game.

Adam winks as he lowers himself down opposite me on the floor.

When we're seated in a circle, Adam leans forward and places his hand on the bottle. "Ten-second kiss. No less."

He spins it, and we wait with bated breath until it slows down and stops on *me*. I fight an eye roll and crawl across the floor, knocking the bottle out of the way.

Adam looks smug in the way only he can be. "Missed me, babe?"

"Not even a little bit," I reply as he slides his fingers into my hair.

He's undeterred, unapologetically crushing his lips to mine. That's when I realize ten seconds can either go by in the blink of an eye or unbelievably slow. Right now, it seems to last forever.

I feel Zach's intent eyes on me as Adam kisses me with hard sweeps of his tongue. It's possessive, the way he used to kiss me back when I was his girlfriend.

I'm lying if I say it doesn't affect me. Kissing Adam brings up suppressed rage I never knew hid in the depths of me. I want to lash out and hit him, but I also want to make him plead for forgiveness. It's a confusing mix of emotions since I don't want him back. Maybe there's a reason why so many people say hate sex is amazing. Right now, I hate him for what he did.

As soon as the ten seconds are over, I tear my lips away and return to my spot next to Jess.

"That was hot," she whispers, giggling.

My lips tingle. I don't want to agree, but how can I not when my palm itches with the urge to crawl back over and slap Adam's smug face.

He doesn't bother to wipe my smeared lipstick off his lips. "Zach, you're up."

As the bottle spins again, I glare at Adam. He stares back with a mischievous twinkle in his blue eyes and a small smile playing over his lips.

I snap my eyes away when the bottle lands on Jess next to me, and a twinge of something ugly rears its head inside me as Zach pulls her in for a kiss.

He doesn't even hesitate. If I thought ten seconds felt long when I was in a lip lock with Adam, I was in for a rude awakening. Jess makes these small, soft sounds of pleasure that causes me to grit my teeth, and his hand is in her hair, tangling in the black strands as he tightens his hold.

I look away, my eyes clashing with Adam.

What a clusterfuck of emotions. When Zach finally leans back, the relief I feel hits me straight in the chest. I can breathe again. My inhales are no longer heavy wings.

I can smell him on Jess when she leans in and giggles, a heady scent that once lingered on my naked skin like an expensive perfume.

"It's your turn to spin, Jess," Adam says, topping up his drink.

Brian holds his empty glass out for more while Jess spins the bottle.

I peer over at the window. It's dark outside now, and with no streetlights around, it looks like the glass has been draped in a thick blanket. The ambient glow of the floor lamp offers just enough light to see by.

"Layla!"

I drag my eyes away from the window. "Sorry, what?"

Brian's smile is too wide for his tanned face. "You're to kiss Jess."

My gaze falls to the bottle seeing that the neck faces me.

A feather-light touch brushes over my cheek, demanding my attention. I let her coax me to her kiss-swollen lips with the tips of her fingers below my jaw. She tastes of strawberry lip balm and vodka, summer holidays, and rebellion.

She breaks away first and begins giggling, her cheeks flushed, her eyes were glazed.

My lips stay pursed for a brief moment longer before I shake myself off and get to my feet. "I need some snacks."

"Okay, that was seriously hot!" Adam points out, jumping to his feet. He's close on my heel, towering behind me like an unshakable shadow.

I grab a handful of chips and bring them to my lips.

"Want to share one of the bedrooms with me tonight?" he asks, brushing my hair aside.

I speak around a mouthful. "Why would I want to do that?"

"We were good together."

I whirl on him. "Were we? Is that why I found you balls deep in that cheerleader?"

He looks sheepish, but I know he doesn't truly regret his actions. Quite frankly, I never realized how much it bothered me until now. "It was a mistake, babe."

I shake my head and brush off my hands. The chips are nice, but the salt and the oily residue are a nightmare to get off. "A mistake is to wear your jumper inside out or call the wrong phone number. Going behind your girlfriend's back to fuck someone else is not. How would you have felt if that was me?"

The reply comes in the form of a muscle ticking in his cheek.

"Why are you even trying, Adam? I thought we were past this?"

He releases a heavy sigh and runs his palm over his mouth. "Look, I made a mistake. A stupid, immature mistake. I like you, Layla. I'm in love with you!"

I blink. Then laugh. "You're in love with me?"

He peers over his shoulder at the others who pretend they aren't listening. When his eyes return to mine, they plead with me not to make a scene. "I'm sorry."

"Don't do this," I whisper. "It's my birthday. Now is not the time."

His hand comes up, and he strokes the back of his fingers over my cheek, his blue eyes flicking between mine. "I'm paying for my mistake every day. How long will you keep punishing me?"

I slap his hand away and walk over to Brian's suitcase to search for more vodka.

Holding up a bottle of white wine, I laugh. "What's this?"

Brian breaks away from Maddy's lips to say, "We're teenagers, Layla. We can't be picky. It was the only bottle I could take that wouldn't raise suspicions with my parents."

I unscrew the lid and take a swig straight from the bottle but freeze with the bottleneck pressed to my lips when there's a thud upstairs. I lower it, looking over at Adam. "Did you hear that?"

It comes again.

His eyes collide with mine. Zach is already up on his feet and walking upstairs. Nothing ever phases him.

I hurry after him, pulling him to a stop on the stairs, whispering, "What if it's a burglar?"

His brown eyes darken, "Then I'll kill him." He turns and walks up another step, but I pull on his arm again.

"Be careful."

He leaves me to stare after him.

One minute passes. My heart is in my ears, pounding loudly.

I hurry after him, up the last few steps and down the long hallway. It's dark except for the soft glow coming from one of the open bedroom doors. The window in front of me has a crack, and when the wind blows outside, you can hear it whistle.

"Zach?" I whisper, creeping silently toward the door.

No answer.

"Zach?" I hiss his name a little louder, looking behind me as a cold shiver runs down my spine.

As I peer into the looming darkness, I feel eyes on me.

I shake myself off and continue forward, slowly. My friends are laughing downstairs, and something tells me this cabin doesn't see occupants often. It feels like a candle warming up a cold, damp basement.

Shadows crawl along the walls as I steel myself and peek inside the bedroom.

Zach looks up from stroking a black and white cat on the bed. "It looks like we have a guest."

I blow out a relieved breath and slump against the door frame. "Jesus Christ."

His brows knit together. "What's wrong?"

I push off the wall and rub my hands down my face as I walk over to him. "Nothing, I just thought…"

He waits me out, dark eyes peering at me from underneath his hood.

"I don't know what I thought." I lower myself down next to him on the bed and stroke the cat behind its ear.

A soft smile plays over my mouth.

Zach gets up and walks over to the door. The lock slides into place, and then he's back, looming over me.

I pause and look up quizzically.

"Adam wants you back."

I don't know what to say, so I say nothing. His nearness makes my breath catch.

"Fuck," he whispers, sounding tortured.

A second passes where he looks at me, trailing his eyes down my body.

"What are you doing?" I ask when he forces me back on the bed, disrupting the purring cat.

He's on top of me, his hand wrapping around my throat, but he doesn't kiss me. Yanking up my skirt, he moves my panties aside and slides his fingers through my folds.

"I can't stop thinking about you," he whispers, circling my swollen clit.

My hips buck. I open my mouth to say something—anything—but he squeezes my throat.

"The way you moaned that night, soft and breathy as not to wake your parents." He plunges a finger inside my tight heat and pumps. "The way your pussy pulsed around my dick."

His fingers dig into my neck, leaving red marks behind. I stare into his brown, dark eyes, my hips rising to meet his skilled touch.

"Do you fuck yourself at night thinking about my mouth on your pussy?"

I nod, my lips parting with a gasp. I'm growing dizzy.

"Adam can't give you what you need."

A shameless moan slips from my lips, and he lets go of my throat to muffle the sound with his hand.

"Eyes on me, Layla."

I fall apart, writhing on the bed as a wave of pleasure floods through me and holds me in its grip while Zach grinds the heel of his hand down on my too-sensitive clit.

When my breathing finally returns to normal, he slides his fingers back out and gets to his feet. "Happy birthday."

Then he's gone, leaving me ruined in the destruction of his burning touch.

CHAPTER 2

"Did you see the cat?" Jess asks when I re-join them in the living room.

It's on her lap, purring loudly and nudging her jaw with its head.

Zach sits on the couch, legs spread, hood pulled low over his face. He doesn't look up from his phone, and I avoid peering over at him.

I'm a terrible friend. Jess likes him, always has, but my clit still tingles from his touch.

"He's cute, isn't he?"

"Yeah," I agree, walking past her to the coffee table. I keep my gaze down as I refill my glass with wine. It's sour but crisp.

"Who's up for another game?" Brian asks from his spot on the armchair with Maddy.

I'm not in the mood. Not for another game. Not for any of this.

"What kind of game?" Jess asks, scratching the cat behind the ear.

"Strip poker," Adam teases.

Brian shakes his head. "None of you fuckers are seeing my girlfriend naked."

Adam goes to reply, but the doorbell sounds.

A hush falls on the room. We exchange a glance.

"Did you invite anyone else, Layla?" Adam asks, his brows pulling low.

"No," I whisper, "I didn't. Did you?"

"No."

I step into the hallway. The front door looms up ahead. I skim my hand over the wall, searching for a light switch but find none.

The doorbell rings again, making me jump. I press a hand over my chest to calm my nerves.

"Are you okay?" Adam asks behind me.

I ignore him. My heart is in my ears, pounding loudly.

I unlock the door and throw it open, expecting to see someone there.

Nothing but empty space greets me.

"What the fuck?" Adam says, perplexed, pushing past me through the door. He steps outside and looks left and right. His breath billows out of him like fog with every harsh breath.

I slowly step out on the damp grass and hug my arms around myself. The night is alive with the sound of crickets. I don't believe in myths and fairy tales, but Maddy's story plays in the back of my mind when I walk up to Adam and pull on his arm.

"Let's go back inside. The bell is probably faulty."

His jaw is tight. He drags his eyes away from the tree line and puts his arm around me. "You're cold."

He's right. Goosebumps line my arms.

I peer briefly over my shoulder as Adam leads me back inside. I could swear someone watches from the shadows.

Adam locks the door and double-checks the windows

too. His anxious nerves make me uneasy. It takes a lot to spook him.

"Who was it?" Maddy asks when we re-join them in the living room.

The sudden urge to close the curtains strikes me then.

"There was no one out there," Adam replies, steering me over to the couch, a hand pressed to my lower back.

Brian echoes my thought. "The bell might be faulty."

Adam pulls me down next to him.

Lodged between him and Zach, I suck in a breath. Both their thighs press up against mine.

"How the hell is a bell faulty?"

"What do you suggest it was then? The bogeyman?"

Zach keeps bouncing his left knee, and I can't look away from the tanned skin peeking out through the rips in his jeans.

"I don't know, but a bell doesn't just go off like that. Twice."

They argue back and forth. I tune out, my attention on Zach's warmth next to me, his fingers flying over his phone screen. I try not to peek, but my treacherous eyes have a mind of their own.

"We need music!" Jess declares, jumping to her feet and startling the poor cat.

My phone pings in my pocket. I fish it out.

Zach: Like what you see?

Me: I'm not looking at you.

Zach: Keep telling yourself that.

Me: Has your ego always been this big?

Ding dong.

I stop typing.

"Does the myth still sound like a joke to you?" Maddy asks, but the quiver in her voice gives her away. She's nervous too.

"It's just a myth," I reply, rising to my feet. Adam goes to stand too, but I motion for him to stay. "I'll be back."

I leave the room and walk down the hallway with determined steps, refusing to look intimidated. The bell must be faulty, like Brian said.

Then why didn't it sound earlier in the day? Why now?

The alcohol has taken effect. I try not to sway on the spot as my hand wraps around the handle. Slowly, I inch the door open and peek outside. Silence greets me. Even the sound of crickets has died down as if the forest is waiting with bated breath.

"Hello?" I step over the threshold, heels sinking into the damp grass. My trembling breath comes in short puffs, visible in the evening air. I hug my arms around myself. There's no one out here, but I'm not alone. I can sense it.

Beyond the trees, a twig snaps.

I stop breathing.

Eyes track me as I take a hesitant step, then another, pulled forward by the darkness.

Goosebumps line my skin from the chill in the air. It's been a warm summer, but autumn is fast approaching, evidenced by the wet leaves beneath my shoes. They stick to my heels with my next step.

Three hooded men step out from the shadows, dressed in black, faces hidden beneath stark, white porcelain masks.

My eyes drift down to the knives in their hands, the long and sharp blades.

My feet move before I know what's happening. I run back

inside the house and slam the lock into place. Adam and the others tumble into the hallway.

"What's wrong?" Adam scoops me up in his arms, and for once, I let him.

"The myth," I say. "It's real."

He stiffens. No one says a thing.

There's a knock on the door, hard and insistent.

I jump and spin in Adams's arms. The knock comes again.

"What's happening?" Jess is trembling with fear.

"Three men," I reply. "Maddy was right."

"Maddy was right about what?" Brian asks.

"They stepped out of the trees with weapons."

"This is ridiculous!" Adam rips the curtain open by the side of the door and jumps back when he comes face to face with a terrifying mask.

The knife in the man's hand glints in the porch light as he taps it on the window.

"What the fuck?" Adam breathes, growing pale.

I tear at my hair. Fear, unlike anything I've felt, beats at my chest, hunting for a way out.

Maddy has started crying. Brian is trying to soothe her. "It'll be okay. It's just a stupid prank."

Only it's not.

"Where did they go?" Adam asks, pressing his face up to the window and peering outside.

A smooth, dainty hand slips into mine. Jess's eyes are glassy with tears, but she holds herself together.

"We need to hide," I whisper to no one in particular.

"No," Adam replies, walking past me. "We need weapons."

Inside the kitchen, he pulls open drawers and scatters their contents on the floor. A butter knife won't get us far, but it's all we can find. The kitchen is empty of anything we can use, almost as if it was designed that way.

A loud crash behind me causes me to nearly jump out of

my skin. Zach and Brian have upturned the coffee table and broke away the wooden legs.

Brian holds one up and says, "At least I can beat them with it if they try anything."

Everything seems to happen around me in a blur, a dense fog I can't see through.

Adam hands me a table leg, and I stare at it in my hand unblinkingly. "Just hit them with it, okay?"

"Okay."

Jess screams next to me, her hand flying up to press over her mouth, her finger pointing to the window.

I follow her line of sight.

A white mask stares back at me through the glass—dark pits of evil where the eyes should be.

Instead of shrinking back in fear, I stride over and pull the curtains shut.

"We're sitting ducks," Brian points out, joining me. He peers outside, his breath steaming the window. "They're gone."

My calm doesn't last long. The front door crashes open, and my worst nightmare comes true when the men fill the doorway, their heads cocked.

Brian shoves me behind him and raises his table leg in the air. "What the fuck do you want?! We don't have any money!"

Jess cries hysterically, and it strikes me as foolish. Fear holds me in its grip, but I refuse to sob and scream and draw even more attention to myself.

Adam steps in front of the girls and holds his table leg up. It's better than the butter knife but not as good as their weapons.

Zach's eyes find mine across the room. He shakes his head infinitesimally. *Don't do anything stupid.*

I narrow my eyes. *Don't tell me what to do.*

Brian beats me by running at the men with his makeshift bat, a battle scream bouncing off the walls.

"Shit!" Zach runs after him.

He's too late. Brian swings at one of the intruders, but they're three against one, and Brian soon has a knife lodged in his side.

I stop breathing when he collapses to the floor, blood soaking through his t-shirt as he coughs up blood.

Zach backs away but gets seized by one of the men.

"Please, no!" I whisper, but my plea falls on deaf ears.

The man in front of Brian bends down, snatches the table leg from Brian's hand, and whacks him.

He raises his arm again.

The club comes down.

It doesn't stop.

The masked man rains blow after blow until Brian's brain lies in thick, mushy clumps on the floor. My hand presses to my mouth, and I release a sob, unable to comprehend the evil in the room. Brian is dead.

Dead.

I'm grabbed and hauled away.

"Walk!"

I'm vaguely aware that one of the men stays behind to guard the others as Zach and I are manhandled up the stairs.

CHAPTER 3

They throw me to the floor with rough hands and tie Zach to the chair while he tries to fight them off.

He can't. He's outnumbered.

The sound of a belt buckle being undone draws my attention back.

"Do you like this girl?" the man in front asks Zach, sliding his zipper down and pulling his big, hard dick out.

"Don't fucking touch her!"

Muffled, amused laughter sounds behind the mask. "She is pretty, I must admit."

Rough fingers drag my bottom lip away from my teeth.

"Such a pretty mouth."

"I'll kill you!" Zach growls, spit flying from his mouth.

Dark eyes peer down at me through the holes in the mask. My knees ache on the floor. "Do you want your friend to live?"

"Please," I sob, unable to stay strong. Not when he drags the flat end of his blade down my cheek and taps my lips with it.

"Suck on my cock."

I shake my head. "Please, don't hurt him."

"I'll think about it if you wrap your pretty lips around my cock like a good little whore while your boyfriend watches."

"You're dead! You're all fucking dead!" Zach thrashes in his chair.

As I begin stroking the man's thick length, it twitches in my hand, and I lean in, taking him in my mouth.

"Good girl," he praises on a hiss, his dark eyes drinking me up. "Just like that!"

His hand in my hair shoves me down until I choke. "Hear that sweet sound, lover boy? How does it feel to watch her gag on another man's dick?"

"You're fucking sick!"

The man doesn't let up. He fucks my mouth with feral brutality, forcing me to take it all.

His bloodied hands smell of copper and death.

"Fuck, I love it when girls cry!" He swipes his thumb through the mascara streaks on my cheek and pulls me off him.

"Good little whore, crawl to my friend and suck his dick too."

The floor digs into my knees as I make my way over to the other man by the door and set to work on his belt while he stares down at me through the mask.

His dick is big and veiny, making my mouth water.

Cum collects on the tip.

I lick it off like a good girl. Somewhere deep inside, a small part of me likes this depravity.

"All the way inside," he whispers darkly, crowning my throat.

I swallow him down and choke, but he holds me there.

I gag again, saliva seeping down my chin.

He slides out and shoves back in, hard. "So fucking good!"

I can't see him through the tears in my eyes, but his stark white mask taunts me.

24

"You want two dicks, princess?"

I'm pulled off, and then they stand with their feet planted, cocks erect, in front of me.

Congealed blood paints the knives in their hands.

"That's it," the man to the left says when I begin stroking their dicks. "Keep doing that."

So, I do. I stroke my hands up and down their thick lengths, my pussy growing wetter with every masculine grunt.

"Are you watching, lover boy?"

The first squirt of cum rains over my face, followed by another. I don't stop stroking until I have milked them of every drop.

It's strange. I feel powerful, in control. But then they abandon me on the floor and press a knife to Zach's throat.

He draws in a sharp breath between his teeth, anger flashing in his eyes.

"What would you do to keep him alive, princess?"

I go to wipe the cum off my face with my sleeve, but the man with the knife tuts.

"Leave it. "

I lower my hand.

A bead of blood trails down Zach's throat.

"What do you want me to do?"

"Bounce on his dick."

"What kind of sick games are you playing?" I cry, shooting to my feet, my hands fisted by my sides. "Isn't it enough that I have your fucking cum on my face?"

"As you wish," he begins sliding the knife across Zach's throat.

I launch myself at the man. "Don't!"

He easily overpowers me and throws me off, the handle of his knife connecting with my temple.

I topple over onto the bed behind me.

"Ride him, or he dies."

I lie sobbing. How is this happening? "It's my birthday," I whisper to myself.

"Consider it a birthday present." To the other man, he says, "Bring the dark-haired girl up here."

Footsteps retreat, then return with a crying, panicked Jess.

She takes in the scene.

Zach's bloodied neck. Me on the bed, my cum smeared face.

She turns in the man's arms and tries to get past, begging, "Please, let me go."

The fear in her voice hurts to listen to, the same way I imagine it hurts a mother to hear her child cry in pain. I want to make it stop.

"Shh, sweet girl, no one will hurt you," the man says, holding her hostage in his big arms, his knife in his hand. "Easy now."

The masked man behind Zach curls his finger at me. "Come here."

CHAPTER 4

I slowly ease my feet down on the floor and stand up from the bed. I feel like I'm walking on water on my way over to Zach. Nothing seems real, a hazy nightmare I will soon wake up from.

"Take his dick out."

Zach's wrists are tied to the chair, and so are his ankles. The knife glints against his throat. A sock has been shoved into his mouth to gag him.

My knees connect with the floor, and I undo his belt and slide down his zipper with trembling fingers.

As I free his dick and stroke the hardening length, I can't look him in the eye. Shame courses through me but not enough to stop me from leaning forward to taste him.

Before I can, a hand in my hair pulls me back. "I said to ride, not suck."

I slowly rise to my feet and climb on Zach's lap, placing my hands on his broad shoulders. My skirt rides up, baring my lace panties and his eyes flick down, watching me slide them aside. His nostrils flare. No matter how angry and scared he is; he still can't help himself.

I guide him to my tight entrance, and the stretch of his thick cock filling me up is delicious.

I try so hard not to moan, but it slips out.

So does his masculine grunt.

Jess continues crying.

"Do you like being inside her, lover boy? Look at the cum on her face! Take a good fucking look at it!" the man orders, fisting my hair and pulling it to the point of pain. To me, he says, "Ride him harder!"

I begin bouncing up and down, faster and faster.

Fuck, he feels amazing.

"Filthy little whore," the man breaths in my ear, his white mask brushing against my skin. He smells of hellfire and danger.

Zach's eyes are intent on me and heavy with pleasure. He tries to hold it off, but he stands no chance tied to the chair. Every muscle in his body tenses up.

I ride him faster, grind my hips harder, and take his release deep inside me. I'm about to come when I'm pulled off and hauled over to the bed, cum leaking out.

The man points his bloodied knife at Jess. "Make your friend come."

When she shrinks into herself, the other man shoves her hard. She stumbles over, her eyes downcast, tears wetting her cheeks.

I feel sorry for her. Panic holds her in its claws and refuses to let go. Ever so slowly, she climbs on the bed.

"Spread your legs!" The man orders me, his head tilted to the side, dark pits for eyes behind that terrifying mask.

My legs fall open, and the nip in the air bites at my swollen sex.

"LICK HER!"

Jess flinches, her eyes closing briefly. She steels herself, leans down, and swipes her tongue through my wet slit.

Sheet fisted tightly in my hands, I make a choked sound. My hips rise off the bed.

She does it again.

I moan.

The men shift closer, dicks straining in their pants, their bloodied knives reflecting off the bedside lamp.

Jess cries out when one of the men fills his hand with her hair and pulls her up sharply.

"You like her sweet taste, slut? How she drips and writhes?"

"Yes," she whispers, shame coloring her cheeks.

He shoves her back down. "Finish her off."

Shaky, warm breaths gust over my sex, and then her lips are on me again, edging me closer and closer to the point of no return.

"Say something filthy to her," one of the men instructs, motioning with his sharp knife.

"Please," Jess cries, her tears mixing with my arousal. "I'm scared!"

"DO IT!"

She lets out a frightened squeal and closes her eyes, fighting to gain control of her shaky breaths heating my tingling clit. "You're a dirty little whore!"

My pussy clenches. I try so fucking hard not to, but my hand lands in her soft hair and pushes her down on me.

"Again!" The man orders.

"I love your tight little pussy."

"Fuck!" I moan, bucking on the bed.

She latches onto my clit and shoves her fingers into me, channeling her fear into every slide, every swirl of her tongue.

"That's it, fuck her harder!"

Jess does. My body rocks on the bed with the next pump of her fingers, and I release a loud cry, pulling on her hair.

I'm riding the edge.

All it'll take is one gentle shove.

My eyes find Zach's across the room.

He spits out his gag and smirks.

I fall.

Down.

Down.

Drowning in a sea of pleasure, tossed on the choppy waves.

When my breathing finally returns to normal, Zach pulls his hands free and bends down to undo the ropes around his ankles. "Fucking prick! You had to tie me for real, didn't you?"

The man to my left laughs. "I should have tied your hands properly and left you."

The ropes land on the floor. Zach rises to his feet, strides over to the bedside table, and kicks it over. He yanks open the drawer. Inside is a long knife with a curved blade.

I scramble back on the bed, my eyes growing wide. "Zach? What are you doing?!"

He takes his time answering. "It's your birthday. We're playing a game." Lightning fast, he strikes Jess in the back and sinks the blade to the hilt.

Blood pours out, a river of red.

He snatches the knife back up and stabs her again and again.

I'm screaming, pressed up against the wall.

It all happens so fast.

Jess's choking, gurgling sounds of fear soon quiet down, but Zach keeps stabbing her, the blade tearing and ripping through her flesh.

Panting harshly, his face splattered with blood, he straightens. A slow smile unfurls on his lips. "Happy birthday, princess."

CHAPTER 5

My hands fly to my mouth, and I shake my head in denial, my eyes darting between Zach and Jess's lifeless body.

Her blood soaking the sheets.

"Didn't see that plot twist coming, did you?" he chuckles, wiping the blade on his hoodie. "That's my favorite part. The moment realization dawns."

My breaths are coming thick and fast, gusting out of me in bellows through my fingers. I squeeze my eyes shut against the rising panic. If I don't get my shit together, I will crumble. Now is not the time to lose control.

I jump off the bed and run for the door, my heart jack-hammering inside my chest.

Heavy feet pound on the floor behind me, followed by an amused, deep chuckle. Arms, slick with blood, band around me and haul me off the floor. "No, no, no. Where do you think you're going? We're not done playing yet."

I let out a scream, but he clamps his hand over my mouth.

"Ssshh! Calm down, princess."

My struggling gets me nowhere.

"Remember the night at the party when I walked you home and fucked your brains out?"

Pitiful sobs rip through me.

"How your tight little cunt squeezed my dick, and how you begged me to fuck you harder."

I try to bite his hand, but he grips my jaw instead, his fingers digging into my skin. "You were so warm and wet and willing."

He's growing hard behind me.

"As you came, I fantasized about slicing your throat and fucking you in your pool of blood."

I tear free and whirl on him, my hand lashing out and striking him across his face.

His knife is in his hand. The blade glints in the soft glow of the bedside light as he wipes a bead of blood from a cut on his lip. "My, my, you do have some fire in you."

I bare my teeth, slowly inching backward. "Fuck you!"

He sucks the blood off this thumb—his own and Jess's—and trails his eyes down my body, assessing me. "Up for a second-round already?"

I spit on him. "Never in a million years!"

He's amused. Wiping my spit off his cheek and smearing the blood in the process, he takes a calculated step forward. "You're not ready to admit it yet, but you love the depraved."

Then he strikes me.

I fall to the floor, and my sobs echo in the small room as he crouches down and raises my chin with the tip of his blade.

The cheap rug scratches at my skin, the knife sends shivers down my spine. I stay quiet, not daring to breathe.

"The rules to this game are simple, sweetheart. You obey me, and I reward you. Cross me, and I punish you. Do you understand?"

When I don't respond, he jostles me. "Answer me!"

"Yes." My voice is quiet, weak.

"Good." He slides his hand into my hair and tugs gently

on the strands before giving a sharp pull. "You'll like this game. I promise."

It's hard to look at him. He's so handsome, dipped in blood and insanity. I hate myself for responding to his cruel touch.

"Yes," he whispers, his hand trailing down to slide around the front of my neck. "We're made for each other. You wait and see." He leans closer, his warm breath heating my skin with every soft exhale. "I'm the fire to your hell."

There's movement in my periphery.

"Tie her up," Zach orders his masked accomplices.

I'm hauled to my feet and dragged to the chair. Long lengths of rope bite into my skin as they tie me up with practiced ease.

Meanwhile, my eyes are glued to Jess's lifeless body on the bed. Her hair, draped over her face, conceals her empty eyes.

She's so still, an empty seashell on a sandy beach, crushed beneath the heel of a boot.

Wake up, please.

CHAPTER 6

"Are you going to be good for me?" Zach looms, a dark shadow, peering down the bridge of his straight nose at me, his leather belt in my face, his cock straining against his jeans.

I drag my eyes away from the visible bulge and swallow.

"I asked you a question," he drawls, his hands coming to his buckle.

It clanks open.

His long fingers inch his zipper down. "Are you going to behave for me?"

My eyes dart to Jess's form on the bed but soon snaps back when he lowers the front of his jeans and boxers.

His veiny, hard dick pops out, a bead of precum forming on the tip.

The cold bite of his blade on my cheek sends my blood rushing south, and I'm struck with the sudden urge to squeeze my thighs together.

Zach strokes his dick while he trails the blunt end of the knife over my parted lips.

"Rule one, I expect an answer when I ask you a question."

I glare up at him and set my jaw, refusing to play along with his twisted games.

He lifts his chin at the masked man behind me, and my head is yanked back, a blade pressed to my throat.

Leaning forward, hands on the armrests, his breath on my lips, he flashes a smile. "Want to die, beautiful? I can make it slow and painful. Ever felt a blade pierce your skin?"

The knife digs into my throat when I swallow down the fear, my heart beating against my ribcage.

"I'll ask you again, princess. Are you going to be a good girl for me?"

A bead of blood forms on my skin and trails down to pool in the hollow between my collarbones. "I'll behave."

"Good," he straightens up and resumes stroking his hard dick, up and down, his hand sliding over the thick length.

My mouth is dry.

"You look hungry, little slut."

I squeeze my eyes shut, so I don't have to watch. My clit tingles, throbbing with need, a deep ache forming between my legs.

Rough fingers force my lips apart and drag over my tongue.

I choke, the knife digging deeper into my skin, the sharp bite sending liquid fire to my core.

"Want to kill her?" Zach asks the intruder behind me, who leans down and hums in agreement. "I can't wait to jerk off to her dying screams."

They're toying with me.

The masked man trails his knife down between my breasts, dipping it into the cleavage of my top. He slices through the strap and tugs down my bra cup.

My breast spills out, my nipple hardening.

He tweaks it while Zach taps my cheek with slick fingers that smell of copper.

"Open your eyes."

My scalp burns when he fists my hair on the top of my head and plants his feet on either side of me, prodding my mouth with his dick.

My lips part; my tongue darts out to taste the precum.

"Little slut," he breathes, his cock disappearing into my mouth.

My wrists strain against the ropes, but I take every inch, a moan vibrating at the back of my throat.

He slides back out, the hard tip grazing my lips, then back in, down my throat. "Suck me just like that. Show me how much you love it."

My other strap is cut, and my top is forcibly yanked down.

Rough fingers pull and tug my nipples until they hurt. The man's white mask brushes against my cheek as he whispers, "We're going to kill you, beautiful. Cut you wide open."

I moan, pulling against the ropes, longing to palm Zach's length and bring him to his knees.

Tied up, I have no choice but to take every delicious inch he feeds me.

I don't complain. Fear and pleasure combined is a sweet, dangerous, and addictive drug. I want more.

I need more.

I moan louder, my thighs pressing against the sides of the chair.

The cock slides back out, a trail of snot and saliva following it.

He slaps me and grips my jaw. "Want more?"

Drugged on him and the masked man's filthy words whispered in my ear, I let out a shameless moan.

"Kill me," I beg, my voice dripping with liquid desire and depravity.

CHAPTER 7

"Not yet," he replies, dipping his thumb into my mouth. Looking behind him, he gestures with the knife in his hand. "Tell Jackson we want the boy up here."

A cold shiver runs down my back, and I try to shake my head no, but Zach slaps me again before soothing the sting with his palm. "What did I say about misbehaving."

Another smack.

I release a crazed laugh. It starts out slow and deep but soon escalates into something feral and dark that creeps out from the shadows. "Slap me again, big boy!"

His answering chuckle coaxes a needy whimper from my lips. "You're playing with fire."

He zips himself into his pants just as the door opens, and Adam is hauled inside.

Downstairs, Maddy sobs.

"See this, Adam?" Zach says, trailing his fingers through the mascara streaks on my cheeks. "Your ex-girlfriend is a whore."

I tear my face away and bare my teeth like a wild, aggressive animal.

"We're playing a game, and you have a choice to make,

Adam." Zach's smile spells trouble. "You see, our little whore wants her pussy filled with cock. I think we should oblige her."

Adam's chest heaves with every breath as he watches Zach walk over to Jess's lifeless body and stroke her bloodied, matted hair off her face.

His eyes flick up. "Either you fuck her, or I'll have my friends here take her every hole."

I never noticed the third masked man enter the room with Maddy.

She's weeping pitifully, her gaze on Jess.

"You want me to rape her?!" Adam spits, his eyes burning with anger and hatred. "You're fucking sick!" Looking around, he adds, "You all are!"

Zach steps away from Jess and cocks his head, a small smile grazing his lips. "Is it rape if she wants it?"

Adam doesn't reply. His eyes track Zach.

"You want it, don't you?" Zach asks me, circling my chair. "You want him to fuck you while we watch."

"What I want is for you to die!" I hiss, painfully aware of my naked breasts and hard, achy nipples.

Zach's smile widens. He motions at me with the knife. "You have a foul mouth." Then his attention is back on Adam. "Did you know I fucked her after she caught you cheating? She came running to me, and let's just say she soon forgot about you when she rode my dick."

Adam goes to charge, but two of the masked men restrain him.

"Feisty," Zach laughs, amused. "What's it going to be? Are you giving her what she needs? What she *craves*," he empathizes, "or are they?"

The masked men.

With my eyes squeezed shut, I fight to control my breathing. I'm scared, aroused, and practically vibrating with adrenaline.

When rough hands undo my ropes, I gasp in surprise and open my eyes.

"On all fours," Zach says to me and leans against the wall, one foot crossed over the other.

Adam stares at me in disbelief and anger as I slide down to the floor and get on my hands and knees.

"Spin around," Zach orders, circling his finger.

I do.

"Pull your skirt up."

I bare my ass to their eyes.

"Push your panties down."

The fabric slides down my thighs until it's stretched taut between my knees. My swollen pussy is on display, a feast for hungry mouths, the folds glistening in the soft glow from the bedside lamp.

I need cock.

Liquid desire seeps out of my clenching heat, a trail of pussy juice begging for a hot tongue to lick it up.

"You've got to three to decide."

The sound of a lighter being clicked open, then the spin of the metal wheel.

"One."

Zach takes a deep pull on the cigarette. Smoke leaks out from his mouth and curls around his face. When he exhales, he says, "Two."

I almost whimper with relief when Adam falls to his knees behind me. Not because he's saved me from being fucked by the three men in masks.

No.

I will finally get relief from this throbbing ache inside me.

"You know what to do."

"I don't think I can."

The embers spark bright orange with Zach's next pull on the cigarette. He flicks the ash and pushes off the wall. "I've seen you fuck girls before. It's not like you to be shy."

Something ugly and sharp stretches its wings.

Zach notices it. Taking a seat on the vacated chair in front of me, he asks, "Did you think your boyfriend only cheated on you once?"

"Shut up!" Adam growls, trembling with anger behind me. "Just shut the fuck up!"

Zach is smiling. He points the sharp edge of the knife at Maddy. "Your friend here is partial to Adam's cock on the regular."

I go rigid.

"You fucking prick!" Adam is livid.

The liquid heat between my legs no longer feels warm. It's cold against my thighs.

The ache is gone.

When I shift onto my butt and look at Adam, he shakes his head, his eyes pleading. "Don't listen to him."

"Is it true?"

His throat jumps. "Babe, no."

I draw my legs up to my body like a shield. "You fucked Maddy when we were together?"

Adam opens his mouth to reply, but Zach makes a 'tsk' noise and says, "Don't lie."

I know it's true when Adam's shoulders slump.

Betrayal.

It tastes bitter on my tongue.

"Maddy?! Seriously? You fucked my friend, you dick!" Then I lash out at him and slap his face, his chest. Again and again. "YOU FUCKED MY FRIEND!"

I'm hauled back and thrown to the floor, my skirt bunched around my waist.

"That's enough!" Zach clicks his fingers at Adam. "Fuck her!"

"No!" Adam's voice is firm.

You can feel the shift in the air. Zach has grown still. "No?"

"I can't do that to her!"

"Gut the girl!" Zach orders the others, waving a dismissive hand at Maddy.

CHAPTER 8

Maddy's frightful squeals are loud in the quiet room when the men seize her and cut her clothes off her body with a knife.

"Fuck! Don't hurt her!" Adam cries out. Then he's on top of me, sliding my panties off my ankles, forcing my legs apart.

"Don't touch me!" I scream, fighting to get away from him.

His hand shoots out and latches around my ankle, and he drags me back down. "They'll kill her!"

I don't want them to kill her, but I also don't want him to touch me. I'm angry and hurt despite telling myself I don't care that he cheated.

He fucked one of my best friends behind my back.

I attack him again, fists and claws, scratching and biting. I'm a monster let loose from my inner shadows.

I'm no match to his big body and heavy weight.

Soon, he's buried to the hilt inside me, my wrists trapped over my head, his hand pressed over my mouth to muffle my screams as he begins moving.

"Sssh, babe! I'm sorry! I'm so fucking sorry!"

I try to buck him off as pleasure builds, and the room fills with the smell of cigarette smoke and copper.

"Fuck." Adam's voice is strangled.

As I continue to struggle, his cock throbs inside me. He can pretend he doesn't want this, but I can see the sickness in his eyes.

The same illness is reflected in mine.

"Feels good, doesn't she?" Zach says almost conversationally, a cigarette hanging from his lip.

When he takes another deep pull and blows the smoke out to the side, he says, "She feels even better when she doesn't want it."

Adam buries his nose in my neck, his hips pistoning against me, his cock edging me closer with every slide.

Zach holds my eyes while he continues smoking.

I'm pinned to the floor like a butterfly, my legs spread wide, my tits bobbing.

I've never been fucked like this before.

Not so brutally and never so selfishly.

I love it.

Adam releases my wrists and flips me over, then fists my hair and takes me from behind, his cock sending shockwaves through my body.

White masks stare back at me.

I grow wetter.

Adam pulls out and milks his dick over my ass, hot strings of cum seeping in between my ass cheeks.

I'm so close.

So close.

Zach tuts and flicks his cigarette over the side of the chair. "You didn't let the lady come."

"I fucked her, didn't I?"

Zach leans back in his chair and regards Adam on his knees behind me.

"First, you cheat on her, fuck her best friend, and then refuse to let her come when you force yourself on her?"

My hand is between my legs, desperately rubbing my hard, throbbing clit.

I'm an animal.

"Look at her. Are you going to leave her like that?"

I moan unapologetically as a wave of pleasure washes over me.

So, so close.

Zach sighs like he's disappointed with Adam and rises to his feet, then kneels behind me as Adam gets dragged away. "Looks like I'll be the gentleman today."

He flips me over on my back and holds me to the floor by my throat, his big hand squeezing. He frees his hard dick, rubs it through my folds—teasing me—and slams his hips home.

My moan comes out choked.

"I fucking love this tight cunt," he groans, taking me slow and thoroughly, dragging every ounce of pleasure from my body until I'm wrung out like a dirty dishcloth.

He's up on his knees, my ankles on his shoulders, his thumb pressing down on my clit. "This is how you like to be fucked, isn't it? Hard and slow while others watch."

He squeezes my naked breasts and rolls my hard nipples between his fingers until I plead with him to stop.

He doesn't.

Maddy sobs somewhere nearby, but I can't hear her from beneath the surface of this river of pleasure. The current carries me closer to the sea.

Closer to sweet oblivion.

"Look at me, my little monster."

I gaze up at him as he moves on top of me, face splattered with blood, his dark hair falling into his eyes.

"Come!"

One word, dripping with darkness, a curled finger from the devil at the threshold to his abode.

Come.

Pleasure tears through me.

I pant and writhe on his cock, wanting him deeper. So fucking deep we become one.

He pulls out, grabs my hair, and brings my face to his dick. "Stick your tongue out."

I stare up at him as he erupts, showering me in squirts of cum.

The first coats my hairline.

The second makes me blink as it spills over my nose and cheek.

The third one rewards me with a taste of him as it hits my tongue.

"Good girl," he groans, the fourth spurt of cum raining over me.

His chest heaves as he stares down at me—at his claiming.

I'm his willing whore.

His queen.

# CHAPTER 9

"She will never forgive you," he says to Adam, the pad of his thumb dragging over my bottom lip.

"You motherfucker!" Adam growls, his body poised to fight. "You always wanted to turn her against me. Don't think I haven't seen how you look at her!"

Smearing his cum over my skin with the tips of his fingers, Zach replies, "You did it to yourself. I provided a shoulder to cry on." He flicks his gaze up and smirks. "A dick to bounce on."

"Fuck you!"

"Rule number two," Zach says, his attention returning to me. "Have fun when you kill." He holds the knife out for me, and I stare at it unblinkingly for a long moment.

"Go on," he coaxes. "Take it."

Sure it was a trick, I slowly wrap my fingers around the handle.

"That's my girl," he praises, his hand sliding into my hair at the nape of my neck.

He pulls sharply as the sound of a struggle ensues behind me. "If you make him scream, I'll reward you." His voice drips with promise.

"I want your cock in my mouth."

I don't even question this side of myself. I'm a starved animal.

I need him to feed me.

His cock swells in his hand as he begins stroking the hardening length. He's a machine.

"How badly do you want me to fuck your mouth?"

I can't look away from his dick and the veins that beg for a lick. My mouth is dry. "Please!"

"Please, what?"

"Choke me with it!"

"If you cut your ex, I'll fill your every hole and fuck you senseless until you beg me to stop!"

When he pulls his jeans back up, I almost cry with disappointment.

His hand wraps around my arm and guides me up to my feet. With a tender touch, he tucks my hair behind my ear and whispers, "I see the devil in your eyes. Let her out to play."

He spins me around and smacks my ass.

My grip on the knife is surprisingly steady as I walk slowly over to Adam.

He struggles against the masked men but falls silent when I stop in front of him and study his face.

"How many times did you fuck her behind my back?" I ask, searching his eyes for the truth.

When he doesn't reply, I peer past his shoulder at my former friend. "How many times did you fuck him, Maddy?"

God, how much can one girl cry? She won't fucking stop.

I give up on Adam and put one foot in front of the other until the smell of her fear and betrayal enters my nostrils, sour and vile. "How many times, Maddy?"

She sobs.

"HOW MANY FUCKING TIMES?!" My scream bounces off the wall, making her flinch.

"I lost count," she whispers softly, weakly.

"You lost count," I echo, wringing the handle in my hand. "Where was I when you fucked my boyfriend?"

Her eyes swim with tears. I like to think they're ones of regret, but we both knew they're not. "Please…"

"Answer the fucking question!"

"You were at cheer practice. Sometimes, you slept next to us in the bed at parties, or he snuck away to meet me in a spare bedroom."

I freeze, a sick feeling settling in the pit of my stomach. "You crawled into our bed and fucked my boyfriend after I fell asleep."

Her voice shakes. "Yes."

I look down at the knife clutched in my hand. Jess's blood has dried on the blade.

My life is a lie. Everything I thought was true has been nothing but deception.

I whirl around and point my knife at Adam. "Did you fuck Jess too?"

Somehow, I know the truth. I don't need him to confirm it.

He fucks everything that walks.

"Oh my god!" I whisper, my hands flying up to my hair. "I've been such a fool!"

Zach chuckles behind me, lighting up another cigarette. Pocketing the lighter, he says, "It gets juicer." To Adam, he continues, "Why don't you tell her about the state championships?"

I sweep my eyes over the masked men. Two stand behind Adam, and the third man is stationed by the door.

There's no escape. I'm not so sure I want to anymore.

"Go on, tell her," Zach repeats, growing impatient.

Adam sighs tiredly and runs a palm over his face before looking at me. "When you traveled away for the competition, I met up with Jess and Maddy."

"No," I breathe, shaking my head in denial. "It's not true."

"I'm sorry."

I look over my shoulder at Maddy. My body follows. "Is it true?"

She doesn't reply, but she doesn't need to. The shame in her eyes speaks for her.

"Oh my god," I breathe, my eyes blurring with tears. "Some friend you are!"

"I'm sorry…"

"Not sorry enough to keep your hands off my boyfriend." I walk up to her and press the knife against her throat. A thrill of excitement shoots through me at the fear I see in her eyes.

"Layla," Adam pleads. "Don't do this!"

"Why?" I hiss, refusing to look away from the panic staring back at me. "Let me guess. You're upset you won't be able to fuck her again if I kill her? What about Brian? He was your friend. Did you get off on fucking his girlfriend behind his back?"

"Toys are always shinier when they belong to someone else," Zach comments, sitting on the chair, one leg slung over the armrest.

I ignore him. He can go to hell too. They all can.

"Any other dirty secrets I need to know? Did you fuck my dad too?"

She shakes her head eagerly.

Big mistake. The blade cuts into her skin, and she inhales a sharp breath at the sting.

Me? I'm staring at the blood trickling down her neck and between the valley of her ample tits in her torn low-cut top. It's a shallow cut, not deep enough to drain her life force.

I want to drag my tongue through the blood and sink my teeth into her skin. It's an urge so intense that my body hums.

I cup her breast, licking a path up to her collarbone, then yank down her bra and take her nipple in my mouth. My tongue swirls and laps, my teeth nip and scrape.

When I lean back, her blood is smeared over my chin. "Say hello to Jess."

Then I slice her throat.

CHAPTER 10

The knife cuts through her creamy skin like butter, and blood begins pouring down her chest in a thick stream. Some of it sprays over my chin and neck, warm and fucking delicious.

I need more of this throbbing excitement coursing through me.

I strike her breast and watch the blade sink to the hilt. Then I stagger back, my wide eyes glued to the knife protruding from her chest as she slides down the wall, a streak of red left behind.

She chokes on her blood, the light slowly fading from her eyes. Death is coming for her.

When her hands fall limp by her sides, I press my bloodied hands over my mouth and release a pained cry.

I killed a person.

Not only that.

I enjoyed it.

I feel Zach behind me, his heat pressing against my back, his fingers brushing my hair off my neck. "There you are, my little monster. I knew you would come out to play."

Adam sobs. It strikes me as weird. I've never seen him cry, and now he struggles to breathe through his blinding panic.

It's pathetic.

I raise my hand and suck the blood off my fingers, one by one.

Then it happens.

A strange sensation starts in the pit of my stomach and spreads throughout my body. I feel sick, feverish. My incisors ache and throb.

Zach tips my head back and drags his thumb over my teeth. "The transition has begun." He sounds excited. Looking over at Adam, he says conversationally, "If Maddy had finished reading the article about the myth, she would've found out that three masked men come to this cabin every year because the legend says the Princess of Darkness will arrive here on her eighteenth birthday."

My hands are in my hair, tugging and tearing, while an intense ache blooms at my shoulders.

"I'm sorry, beautiful. It will be over soon." Then he continues with his ridiculous story. "Do you know what you are? You're a demon, Layla. A demon, hidden in the human world to keep you safe until your powers manifest. You're not just any demon though—you're the devil's daughter. The rightful successor to his throne."

"You're fucking insane!" Adam growls behind me. "You need to be locked up in a fucking mental hospital somewhere."

Zach ignores him, his fingers on my jaw coaxing me to turn and look at him.

"The transition starts when she kills. Think of it like sowing a seed. It's not complete yet. First, you must quench your thirst, that for sin and that for nourishment."

There's movement in the room, the sound of heavy feet

on the floor. Strong hands stroking over my back, my shoulders.

Zach steps back.

The three masked men close in around me, their hands roaming, grabbing.

"In my world," Zach says, hidden from view by the broad chest in front of me, "sex infuses you with power. For someone like you, Layla—a true princess—power is a sweet, tempting drug. It's food. You need it to survive."

My boobs are squeezed, and my nipples are tweaked.

Hands slip between my legs and dip inside my skirt to stroke my wet sex.

Zach's voice sounds far away. "At the taste of first blood, the transition shall begin. Watered with the seed of hell, her wings shall sprout. An eruption, a birth of power so strong even the fires of hell shall burn brighter."

Everything is spinning.

Stripped out of my clothes, I'm guided down to the floor, where we become a mass of writhing bodies and moans. Their clothes come off, but their masks stay on.

Bottomless pits stare back at me.

I know I'm not ready to see what hides beneath. Something is growing inside me, flexing its limbs.

Without clothes, the men are a mass of muscle and tattoos. Intricate symbols and swirling patterns.

I'm lifted like I weigh nothing and placed on a lap, my nails digging into the man's chest.

Sinking down on his hard cock, my head falls back. The ache in my incisors grows until I snarl a feral sound that causes the man beneath me to curse excitedly and grab me by my throat as I roll my hips.

The masked men are everywhere.

Beneath, in front, behind.

When a cock presses up against my lips, I obediently open my mouth, my pussy clenching around the dick inside me.

"Jackson, complete the second stage," Zach orders.

Pain sears through me as the third man works his thick length inside my ass, inch by inch, until I feel them everywhere.

Moving, pumping, cursing. We're a symphony of pleasure.

"Are you looking, Adam? By taking her, they're setting the second part of her transition into motion. Trust me. You'll like what happens next."

I gag on the dick in my mouth, my eyes on the white porcelain mask. He's rough, merciless.

They all are.

"Such a sweet, fucking ass!" Hands squeeze my creamy globes, then smack them hard.

Cocks slide in and out, fast and slow. Hard and brutal, coaxing my desire to flow down my thighs.

The wet sounds emanating from my pussy mix with slapping skin and snarls.

I want to pull away and hiss like a street cat.

Zach lights up another cigarette, the smoke escaping out of his mouth before he inhales it. I can see him out of the corner of my eye as he watches the scene unfold in front of him.

He's calm, waiting patiently for it to play out.

"Do you know how a royal is birthed in my world?" he asks Adam, slowly walking the length of the room. "First, she has to kill. It births the hunger for death and pain. You see, a seed from the devil himself is a true monster, worse than any demon or fae you could imagine." He points his fingers with the cigarette pinched at our orgie. "Then she needs to be filled with the nourishment of hell, fucked by true demons." He laughs and takes another pull on his cigarette. "Don't look so disgusted. It's normal in our world. You'll soon see the most beautiful fucking thing you'll ever witness. Layla here is not simply a demon, but part fae too."

"Mmmmh," I moan around the dick in my mouth, my chin smeared with blood, saliva, and snot. I'm starving.

"I know," Zach says behind me. "They'll soon give you what you need, beautiful."

My eyes flutter close—every muscle in my body tenses. The pain in my ass has been replaced with pleasure, and I arch against the man with every thrust.

They move in tandem, stretching me, filling me.

"Dirty whore," the man beneath me whispers, his stark white mask staring up at me. He pinches my nipple, and I pull away from the cock in my mouth to release a fierce snarl.

Zach appears in front of me and grabs my jaw. He's rough, angry. "Bad girl! What did I say about behaving?"

I bare my teeth, staring up at him through a haze of red.

Meanwhile cocks keep stealing my breath, pounding into me with such force I rock into Zach.

"Look at that," Zach says with awe in his voice as he presses against my incisor with his thumb. It comes away with a bead of blood forming at the tip. Then he steps back and motions to the man by his side. "Finish it. She's close."

The cock is back in my face, slapping my lips. "Open up."

I moan around the thick length and take as much as I can until my throat constricts.

"Shit!" he growls, pulling out and slamming back in.

I gag and choke.

He doesn't let up.

None of them do.

I climax so hard it's a miracle I survive this unearthly experience of having my soul torn from my body and shattered into fragments that paint the sky like stars.

Loud masculine groans rise to a crescendo.

The first spurt of release coats the back of my throat, and I greedily drink it down. Every last delicious drop that squirts into my mouth.

Ragged breaths and bodies slick with sweat.

I am ruined.

CHAPTER 11

They shift me and step away.

Cum leaks out of my pussy and ass as I let out an anguished cry and push up on my hands. The space between my shoulder blades burns fiercely as though gasoline has been poured there and lit on fire.

I cry out and collapse, my forehead pressed against the floor. I writhe and convulse until a hush falls on the room.

"Watered with the seed of hell," Zach says, his voice filled with awe.

Something shifts behind me, parting the air in the room.

Something large and heavy.

A black feather falls to the floor in front of me, and with the next shift behind me, it floats up and away.

"Isn't she magnificent?"

"Layla?" Adam asks, horrified.

I'm transfixed by the shadow that moves across the floor with every heavy shift behind me.

I rise to my feet but release a startled scream when the floor lamp crashes to the ground and descends the room into darkness.

Zach appears in front of me as one of the men switches

on the roof light. "It's okay. Don't be scared." He slowly walks around me and drags his palm over a large wing that spans half the room.

They jerk at the odd sensation and knock over picture frames on the chest of drawers.

I scream again.

What the fuck is happening? Turning in a circle, I try looking behind me, but the wings move with me.

The men duck down.

Zach rushes to catch up and cups my cheeks, his touch tender and soothing. "Layla, it's okay. You have wings. Don't be scared."

I bounce my eyes between his, unable to comprehend what he's talking about. I have wings?

No.

"You should see yourself. How beautiful you are."

I shove him away and step back but startle at the feel of the feathers brushing up against the wall to my side. The wings flex, and I cry out.

"It'll take you some time to gain control of them."

"They're so big," one of the men behind me comments, his dark pits wide beneath his mask.

"I told you this one was special," Zach agrees.

The air is sliced again, and I realize the wings flapped, but they are still wide and outstretched.

I try to turn and look at them again, but they follow like a shadow.

Zach chuckles. "They're attached to you."

"Stop messing with my fucking head!" I spit.

Zach claps his hands together. "I forgot to tell you about the best part, Adam." He sounds so fucking excited. I'm still turning in a circle, trying to see the wings behind me.

The men duck again as one of my wings sweeps by overhead.

"Any minute now, the hunger will set in."

I pause, looking up at Zach. "Hunger?"

He smirks. Crossing the small room, he begins circling Adam. "At the taste of first blood, the transition shall begin. Watered with the seed of hell, her wings shall sprout. An eruption, a birth of power so strong even the fires of hell shall burn brighter." He pauses for effect, his eyes locked on mine. "A *hunger* so fierce, the sinners in the pits of hell will be consumed by it. She's to feed on the flesh of betrayal to finalize the transition." He looks over at Adam and flashes an amused grin. "Flesh of betrayal, Adam. Get it?"

Another shift and a flap vibrate through me.

I whimper.

Zach gives me a patient, kind look. "You'll get used to them."

"Do they have wings?" I ask, pointing at the naked, masked men. Why am I even asking? This is some elaborate, sick joke.

"No, they're demons. You're part demon and fae. The wings are courtesy of your mother, the queen of fae."

"The queen of fae," I mumble, unable to take in all this nonsense. "My mom works in a supermarket, Zach. My father is an accountant. This devil and fae talk is ridiculous."

"Is it?" he says with a smirk, his brows raised.

My wings flap again.

Adam is white as a sheet. He looks like he might pass out any minute.

"Has the hunger started yet?"

I go rigid. That wasn't my own thought.

Zach inspects his nails. "Fae can communicate with their mind."

He's fucking insane, I think, distracted by another feather that comes swirling and whirling to the floor in front of me.

Lowering his hand, Zach tuts. "It's not very nice to call me insane."

I snap my eyes to his.

"Not only can fae communicate with their minds, but they can read thoughts too."

"Stop doing that!"

His smile is impossibly wide. He enjoys this.

I start to reply, but all my senses hone in on Adam. Suddenly aware of his racing heart and the blood coursing through his veins, my mouth waters.

I step toward him, my head tilted to the side as I listen to his heartbeat.

His quickening breaths.

"I can smell your fear," I comment, pausing as something sharp grazes my bottom lip.

I reach up, prodding my teeth.

I have fangs, for lack of a better word.

I poke them again.

Am I a vampire?

"You're not. It's the devil in you."

Adam's heart thunders like hooves, making my teeth ache and throb.

Another step closer.

"What the fuck is this?" Adam's voice is panicked.

Good question.

My feet move, padding on the floor. "I can taste your fear on the air."

"Get away from me!"

"Your blood pumping through your heart, the sound of it swishing." I cock my head again, listening.

Another step closer. Adam is within reaching distance.

He steps back, and I follow his retreat until the wall is pressed against his back. He doesn't know it, but his fear makes the hunt sweeter, like the smell of your favorite dish on the stove when you're hungry.

"Are you scared, Adam?"

His jaw is tight. "Fuck you!"

My wings flex. I trail my gaze over his face and neck, my eyes lingering on his pulse point.

Thump.

Thump.

It flutters against the skin. My teeth tingle and ache.

"Oh, Adam," I breathe, my palms sliding up his muscular chest, my pussy clenching around nothing.

He shoves me off, but I grab his throat, surprised at my own strength when I tear his T-shirt and drag my nails down his chest.

Blood rushes to the surface, beading on the skin, a single drop slowly inching closer to where his happy trail disappears into his jeans.

"Betrayal," I whisper, "You reek of it."

It's everywhere like a heady, overpowering aftershave. I've been blind to it before, but now I can smell it on him.

The women.

Every feminine moan he's swallowed lingers on his deceitful tongue. Every bite of teeth on his collarbone as he pounded his flavor of the week.

I lean in and drag my nose over his neck, breathing in his lies. "You came on Jess's face."

It's impossible to describe, but I can smell and taste the truth on him.

"You fucked Maddy in the driver's seat of your car in my driveway while I was home because you got off on the thrill."

A trill laugh of mine dances across his skin. "You only fucked Jess because she wanted Zach, and you knew he wanted me. It was a big fuck you!"

I move back and wag my finger. "Naughty boy!"

The floor is cold beneath my knees as I drop down and tear at his belt, his buttons.

His jeans slide down his thighs. I palm his length and give it a stroke.

Despite his fear, it hardens.

I smile up at him through my fangs; my eyes are red pools of hellfire that flicker and dance. Behind me, my wings stretch out. "I'm hungry, Adam. I'm so fucking hungry it consumes me."

His cock hasn't got the memo that he's the meal at this banquet.

I rise to my feet and continue stroking his dick, my thumb swiping over the bead of precum collected in the slit.

His ragged breaths, his half-mast eyes. I don't miss a thing.

His tongue darts out to sweep across his bottom lip, and I snatch it up between my teeth and suck it into my mouth.

His cock twitches in my hand.

I jack him hard and fast. Eager to get him off.

I'm playing with my food and toying with my mouse. Adam is a condemned prisoner fed his last meal.

"Fuck!" he groans deliciously when I release his tongue. Blood seeps from the corners of his lips. I grazed him with my teeth.

Zach is nearby, watching and waiting, a cigarette dangling from his lips, smoke swirling in the air.

"Betrayal," I whisper, my lips brushing up against Adam's neck. "It smells so sweet."

His body tenses, and warm cum spills onto my hand and rains over my belly.

I strike, my teeth tearing and ripping through flesh. After spitting the large chunk of tendons on the floor, I attack again, feeding on his screams and the warm, gushing blood.

My wings stretch out to their full glory behind me as I tear out another piece of flesh.

His screams soon die down, and his body slumps to the floor, twitching.

I'm on him, shielding my kill with my wings as I feast and drink, a feral animal full of snarls and growls.

The last of my humanity is burned away by the fiery pits of my darker nature.

I can feel it.

The power.

It thrums through my veins, a calling to my immortal parents.

Their daughter has arisen.

The question is? Who will claim me first?

CHAPTER 12

I unfurl my wings and peer at Zach and the demons.

"You're fae?"

Zach crushes his cigarette beneath his shoe. "Correct."

"They're demons?"

"Also correct."

I crawl off what's left of Adam, my body soaked with blood, strips of flesh stuck between my teeth.

My eyes bounce between the men in front of me. I sense danger, prey in the presence of predators.

Zach cocks his head, an amused smile playing on the left corner of his mouth. *"Where are you going, princess?"*

"My parents don't get along." It's a statement.

The masked men advance, calculated slow steps.

"They don't," Zach confirms, that smirk still intact.

"But they left me here in the human world to protect me until my powers came in."

Zach hums, pushing off the wall. "They did."

A veil has been lifted. "You found me before my birthday. You're new at the school." My eyes snap up. "You suggested I should rent a log cabin for my eighteenth birthday."

He hums, advancing slowly. *"Also true. I thought it was fitting with the legend."*

I hiss, barring my teeth, my eyes changing from red to black.

The men pause.

"It's okay. The transition isn't complete yet. She's still weak. We need to restrain her and cut her wings."

"What we need," one of the masked men says, "is to get out of here before they come for her. Can you not sense it? They're coming."

Zach shrugs one shoulder and steps past the men. He's in front of me now, crouching down. "There's no need to be afraid. We want your power, that's all."

When he reaches for me, I release a fierce snarl and snap my wings shut behind me.

His hand retreats. "You're a beautiful creature. The world has never seen something like you before, born of the devil and the fae."

He rises to his feet and circles his finger in the air. "It's time to get this show on the road."

The men advance and haul me to my feet, but the fire in my stomach grows and spreads until, out of instinct, I shoot my hand out, a ball of fire floating in the air in front of me. It's small at first until it grows taller and spreads, encompassing me. When I move, it moves with me. I'm immune to the heat.

"I thought you said she was weak," one of the men asks, his porcelain mask visible through the flames.

"She is."

"Are you blind? A wall of fire surrounds her. Not just any fire, but hellfire."

Zach looks annoyed, as if I'm a bothersome child.

My flames soon flicker and die.

"That's why she's weak. She can't sustain her magic for long. Not yet."

He shoulders past the men and hauls me to my feet, his touch rough, punishing. "Let's go!"

Magic swirls out of me effortlessly like it wants to protect me, and the men double over and grip their heads. One runs for the window and slides it open.

Zach's sharp voice rings out, "ENOUGH!"

My magic races back inside me.

The men slumps.

Zach slaps me hard and digs his fingers into my jaw. "If you ever use terror on my men again, I will hurt you!"

I snarl.

"You have so much of hell in you," he says, studying my face. "But I can sense your fae too." He scans his eyes over my wings as they unfurl behind me. "You do that when you feel threatened," he observes, "like an animal that makes itself appear bigger to its enemy."

"Have you ever seen such big wings?" one of the demons asks.

Zach shakes his head and steps around me, my wing spanning out over his head. "I've never met anyone of her breeding."

"Her existence throws the realms out of balance."

"Or brings them *into* balance," Zach murmurs, reaching up to stroke his hand over the feathers, but I snap my wings shut, barely missing his face.

"Impressive."

"What do you want with me?"

His eyes find mine. *"To cut your wings and drain you of your power."*

"How do you do that?" I ask out loud.

"Your power is in your wings and your blood. The bigger the wings, the more powerful you are."

I walk around him and approach the men, careful to ensure I have them all in my sights. "How did you know where to look for me?"

"We didn't," Zach replies. "But if you torture the right people, you soon find out. It wasn't difficult. I expected all along that you were made a changeling."

"How so?" One step closer to the open window.

"Your parents had to make snap decisions. It would be too dangerous for you to grow up in hell. The world of the fae was dangerous too. *But here...*Enemies wouldn't think to search for you in the human world."

The evening breeze coming in from the window lifts my hair off my shoulders. The room looks like a horror scene with dead bodies scattered everywhere and blood sprayed over the walls.

Happy birthday to me.

CHAPTER 13

I center myself and inhale deeply before sending all my power out in one hard stream through my hand.

The entire side of the house blows off.

I scream, unprepared for the explosion of sound and debris that shoots up in the air and rains back down.

Zach begins laughing behind me, but I'm bewildered. I can feel the magic thrum in my veins. My skin's hair stands on end with the power flowing through me.

I was still not prepared for it, though.

"Impressive, but destructive."

I don't wait around. Everything that happens next is instinct. *Get to safety,* my brain whispers.

I dash for the outside world, and my wings spread out and flap, lifting me off the ground. There's a knack to this, and I haven't mastered it.

I stare down at the roof of the house beneath me, the top of the trees.

Zach pulls his hoodie off and jumps out after me, black wings erupting from his back. "Where are you going?" He's skilled at flying. I'm not.

"Is this real?" I ask, my eyes wide. This morning I was an average teenage girl. Now I'm flying high up in the sky.

"Who knows what's real," he replies with a smirk and shoots both hands out, shifting the wind and the air.

I tumble to the ground and hit the grass with such force that the oxygen leaves my lungs.

"Sucks to be immortal, doesn't it?" Zach comments when his feet land next to me. "I can torture you for hours and days, and you won't die."

"Fae can die," I point out as I jump to my feet and attack him. We fall to the ground and roll, him on top of me.

"Fae can die," he confirms. "You're not all fae."

I lift my head off the ground and sneer in his face. "But you are!"

The surprised, choked sound he makes when he looks down and sees my hand lodged inside his chest causes a tinkling laugh to bubble up inside me.

I slip my hand back out, his beating heart clasped tightly. "How long until it stops?" I ask, piercing the flesh with my long nails.

My incisors grow.

Zach chokes, blood pouring from between his lips.

I bring the heart up to my nose and breathe it in. It's slowing down. "You were wrong about the legend. She ends up feasting on the betrayal of fae and demon. The very essence that birthed her and abandoned her in the human world to cause destruction and death."

I sink my teeth into the flesh and moan with pleasure as it ceases beating. It's still warm, blood pouring from the chambers as I tear off a chunk.

Zach is a dead weight on top of me.

I can sense the others watching nearby, their fear potent in the evening air.

Zach's body rolls off me with a thud, and I get up on my knees, beckoning them to me with a curled finger.

Three masks land on the grass. Dark pits, flickering with the flames of my father's throne, gazed down at me.

Traitors.

I swipe my tongue over the blood on my bottom lip and begin stroking their thick cocks.

"Are you going to be good boys for me?"

Their sharp teeth gleam in the soft silvery moonlight.

"Yes, princess."

I lean forward and take one of the glorious cocks in my mouth while stroking the other two. Moaning, I bob up and down on his length.

Hands are in my hair, pulling and fisting.

I suck harder, stroke faster.

When they finally tense and groan, I release the cock in my mouth with a pop.

As their seed showers me in delicious warm spurts, my head falls back, and I smile up at the moon, drawing its power into me, the tide, the wolf's howl.

I'm starving.

Cum slides down my neck and drips off my tits. It's on my skin, in my hair.

I'm a painting of sin, a clean canvas splattered with blood, gore, and sex.

I'm my father's daughter.

My wings unfold slowly, their magnificence taking the demons by surprise and coaxing gasps from their lips.

In a flash, I'm on them, tearing them to shreds, my wings slowly coming down to shield my kill from prying eyes while I feast.

CHAPTER 14

"Layla, what the fuck?!"

"LAYLA!"

I stare unblinkingly down at the table leg in my blood-smeared hands.

Brian's battered face is unrecognizable, and chunks of his brain stick to my hair and clothes.

"What the hell did you do?"

Maddy is sobbing. They all are.

I stagger back and fight to control my breathing. What the fuck happened? I'm dressed. I don't have wings.

Zach stands with Jess in his arms, a look of horror on his face.

"He's dead," Adam whispers.

I try to make sense of reality, but I'm so fucking confused. The table leg clatters to the floor. I fist my hair and shake my head. "There was fire."

Adam swallows thickly, his eyes on the dead body on the floor. "Layla, you need help."

"You fucked my friends!" I drop my hands, only to realize there's a knife in one. When the fuck did I pick it up? I point it at Adam. "You fucked Maddy and Jess!"

He frowns. "What?!"

"You fucked my friends when I was at the state championships!"

"Layla, please put down the knife," Zach says in a soothing voice, letting go of Jess and approaching me with his hand held out, palm face up. "Drop it to the floor. No one else has to get hurt."

I run over to the window and rip the curtains open. "There were masked men."

Nothing but darkness.

"There's no one out there."

"They wore porcelain masks and had sharp teeth." I let go of the curtain and motion to Brian on the floor with my knife. "They killed him!"

One step closer. Zach has a look of regret on his face. "No, *you* did. You killed him, Layla."

I blink, then look past him at Brian's lifeless body. "No…"

"Drop the knife."

I hold it out, my arm steady. "Don't come any closer!"

"Okay," he says, holding his hands up placatingly.

I inch past him, closer to the others. "Did you like fucking my boyfriend?" I hiss at Maddy.

She shrinks back. "I haven't fucked him. I would never do that to you!"

A trill laugh dances on my lips. "Brian's cock wasn't enough. You had to go behind my back too."

I whirl on Adam and Zach when they try to advance. "Don't you fucking dare!"

"Babe," Adam whispers, taking a step closer. "Look at me. Why would I cheat on you with your best friends?"

"Why would you cheat on me at all?" I counter.

He's closer now. One more step, and he'll be within reaching distance. "It was a mistake!"

I can feel the phantom weight on my back, but there are no wings. I miss them, even though they were never mine.

Another delusion.

The doctor holds out a small bottle of pills. "You must take these. One tablet twice a day."

"What are they?" I ask the man in white as I accept the medicine bottle. My name is printed on the front.

His bald head shines beneath the fluorescent light. "Antipsychotics."

I swallow thickly. "What happens if I don't?"

He hesitates a moment before whispering, "Bad things."

"Where are the men?" I ask. "They were here!"

"How many times do I need to tell you there are no men."

I flick my eyes between his uncomprehendingly.

The last step is erased. His fingers stroke over my cheek. "We can get you help."

"I don't want help," I reply, shoving the blade into his gut. "I don't need shrinks prodding me and locking me in a padded room. Do you know how slowly time passes in there?"

His face is pained. Blood pours from the corners of his lips.

I slip the knife back out and stab him again, higher up this time. Then again.

Vaguely aware of the screams in the room, I remove the knife and strike the side of his neck.

Blood spurts.

"I don't want to go back there!"

The air shifts with the phantom weight of my wings.

Adam collapses to the ground, the light gone from his eyes.

I stare down at him for a long moment before laughter sounds in the room.

It's my own.

Blood trails a path down the knife's handle and over my hand when I hold it up in front of my face.

Whimpers bring me back to the here and now. Maddy and Jess cower against the wall while Zach stands motionless off to the side, his eyes locked on Adam's lifeless body and the pool of blood spreading across the floor.

"How many times did you crawl in my bed and fuck him when I was asleep?"

Maddy looks confused. "What are you talking about? Layla, you're not making sense."

I walk over to my backpack and unzip the inner compartment. My fingers brush over cold metal.

Their eyes widen at the gun in my hand.

"Where did you get that?" Jess asks as Zach steps forward and holds his hand out. "Easy, Layla. You don't want to do this."

"Fuck you!" I hiss at him! "You want to steal my powers!"

He swallows.

"You can't have my wings!"

"Okay," he soothes, "I don't want your wings."

"Bullshit!" I take aim.

The girls cry louder. I want to command them to shut up! Either that or blow their brains out.

"On your knees!" I order Zach.

He obeys, his hands clasped behind his head.

I close the small distance between us and press the gun to his head. "I let you fool me once. I'm not letting it happen again. How did you find me?"

"Find you?" he asks.

"In the human world?! Don't lie to me!"

"Layla," he breathes, but I dig the gun in harder.

"I told you not to lie!"

"Babe, you're sick. You need help."

I let out a scream and fire at the wall behind his head, making him flinch, and the girls scream. "I AM NOT SICK!"

He breathes harshly, his broad chest expanding with every inhale.

I step behind him and use the knife to cut open his hoodie and t-shirt. It rips through the fabric.

Inspecting his back and shoulder blades, I let out a frustrated sound and say, "Where are they? How do you get them to erupt?"

"What are you talking about?"

"YOUR WINGS?!" I'm prodding him hard, my nails digging into his perfect skin. There's not a mark on him.

"I don't have wings!"

I crouch down and drag the knife down his shoulder blade in hunt for his elusive wings, ignoring his pained cry. I've seen them with my own eyes. They're black like mine but smaller. He's fae.

Peeling back the skin, my fingers sliding across flesh and muscle, I see no wings, no feathers.

I step back, heavy breaths gusting out of me as I stare at his bleeding back, his skin in two flaps.

He's pale.

So pale.

"Oh god!" Maddy whimpers, mascara streaks down her wet cheeks. Is that what she looked like when she sucked off Adam?

I raise my gun and fire a shot, fed up with her goddamn whining.

Jess releases a scream and presses her hands to her ears.

Blood gushes from Maddy's abdomen. She looks down and releases a frightened sob, so I shoot her again, then scratch at my temple with the gun.

"Have you always been this fucking annoying?"

Dark red blood splutters from her lips as she coughs.

Jess runs for the door.

I shoot her too, bored with the drama.

This weekend has gone to shit. At least no one will cut off my wings.

I feel their weight behind me.

My feet carry me over to Jess.

She crawls away from me and presses up against the wall, a trail of blood in her wake.

I follow it like Hansel and Gretel followed the pebbles home. "I thought you were my friend." I sink down on my haunches and cock my head. "Friends don't fuck each other boyfriends."

She whimpers as I brush her hair away from her pale, frightened face. "But then again, I fucked Zach, so maybe we were never really friends."

I fucking love the gurgled sounds she makes when I set to work with the knife, stabbing her again and again until the muscles in my arms burn with exertion.

I collapse to the floor, out of breath.

What a rush!

Maddy is still alive, but barely.

Cold metal presses to the back of my head. "You shouldn't have left your gun unsupervised." Zach's voice is deep and controlled.

I laugh. It's too funny not to. "Looks like you'll get my wings after all."

"Get up!"

I slowly rise to my feet, smirking at him, my hands held up in defeat.

He grabs my arm and hauls me upstairs, where he throws me down on the bed. The same bed where he killed Jess.

But I killed Jess.

My head is a mess.

He removes his leather belt and secures my wrists to the

bed frame, then presses the gun to my forehead, his knees on either side of me. "I should blow your brains out."

I try my restraints. They're secure.

"Do it!"

His deep chuckle sends shivers down my back as he pulls the black hoodie over his head and tosses it to the floor. Then he removes his t-shirt and forces it into my mouth.

Magnificent black wings sprout from his back.

"That would be no fun."

The End.

ACKNOWLEDGMENTS

Firstly I want to thank *you* for reading this little short story. You've made my day.

Also a big thank you to Paula. Thank you for being you!

My hubby. Thank you for reading everything I write even though it's not science fiction. I know you live in hope that I will one day write a book about epic space battles. Keep dreaming.

Brit at ThisBitchReads for editing this novella. Thank you, lovely.

Harleigh.

Also by Harleigh Beck

ABOUT THE AUTHOR

Harleigh Beck lives in a small town in the northeast of England. When she's not writing, you'll find her head down in a book, munching on something undoubtedly unhealthy. She mainly reads romance, but she also likes the occasional horror. She has more books planned, so be sure to connect with on her social media for updates.

Printed in Great Britain
by Amazon